Love Is Blind, But the Neighbors Ain't

MaryAnn Hayatian

ButterflyAnthology

www.butterflyanthology.com

Family
thank you for giving
support I needed
when I aspired to have my accomplishments
completed
Dad

Miss you

It is the weekend of an early spring afternoon, in the city of Montreal, the day cannot result to a squander.

I'm in a rush actually, I have to meet the gang on the corner of Sherbrooke Street near where the three bedroom duplex I live in, stood still. I live with my parents, my older sister, and younger brother.

I'm currently attending SGW University, too eager on getting my advertising degree and becoming a promoter, update everyone with new things in this life we see.

That was my introduction.

The gang's and my mission today, is to focus on our friend James performs with his band, the EternalCryzz in a play, at a nearby theater downtown.

James is my next door neighbor, I knew him since I was five years old.

I'm trying to dress up quickly, while walking back and forth in my bedroom I share with my sister Hayley, picking up the shirt from the floor, which I wore last night, it seems better to wear it today.

I ran downstairs, locked the front door, and walked to the corner where

Celia, an excellent friend of mine since high school, had already set there waiting for me. Celia is very smart, slim and tall.

She has long brown hair, up to the end of her back and gray eyes that look invisible from the glare of the sunlight. Her passion is math, yes, it's hard to believe, but that's her gift. She has a twin sister, an opposite rude and sloppy. Identical in features, but her hair color is pitch black.

"Hey, Lynna!" she said.

"Hi."

"Originally we have to be late, Syd has not arrived yet!" We started to giggle.

"Celia, it must've taken forever to get his hair into place!"

Syd is a friend of James, a greased haired know it all, but a cool guy.

Their friendship began in summer camp, James was ten years old, and Syd was twelve.

Syd is a prankster. Kids called him a clown back then, a real tall one. His parents own all sorts of buildings.

They bought a theater near the Old Montreal area a couple of months ago, and registered it on his name, so he can start a career of something. "You will be a fine business manager one day, son." His father had told him when Syd had just turned thirteen, while he was in his puberty phase. It seemed already planned. However, his father had some doubts to trust him, he had asked James to be Syd's partner, and of course, James would not turn it down.

This would be a great start for James' profession. He is a musician, but in his own world, he calls it rock star. That place would be the entertainment for

Syd. His duty would be planning parties, plays, and concerts. This is his dream, I guess.

The name of the place has not been revealed yet. Perhaps it would be called Syd's Palace.

Syd finally arrived to pick us up in his mini red 1970 something convertible. He lives uptown, about fifteen minutes away from here.

"You're late!" Celia said, with a disappointing tone in her voice, while she and I went to sit in the back seat of the car and I was closing the door.

"I'm not sorry, were you two freezing out there?" he said sarcastically.

It is not exactly a warm spring yet in early April.

"Not really, the cold weather is starting to disappear in this part of the city. You must be still freezing uptown."

"Poor girls, how did you walk in this pain?" "Easy, we ran." I said.

He laughed, it more sounded like little bubbly chuckles were coming out of his mouth.

"How's the theater operation?" I changed the subject.

"Good, I just received the business license with my name on it." "That must be hard to get."

"No way man! You go to that registering place, and get yourself a company name."

"Which is?" Celia asked.

"Now it's not the time to say it," he answered. "What kind of name is that?"

"I meant you will know it, once the place is open."

"You need to inspect that place, and make sure mice are not around." "The theater's clean."

 "Make sure of that, don't want to frighten the guests away, do you now?"

"I know what's going on, thanks for the notice Madams," he said.

I know he said that, to both shut us up, until we got to the theater.

Everything is sarcasm to Syd, if you joke and try to imply something at the same time, he has the tendency to stop you and make you feel bad. He likes to be the joker, it's a Syd thing as I put it.

We arrived at the parking lot beside the theater. The place was already packed with cars.

"Syd, there's one!" Celia shouted, as she was pointing at a spare parking space in the back of where we were.

"Ok, ok."

He had to reverse and go to the second row.

We entered in the old brown Medley Theater, where there is a large sign that says, Live it up with EternalCryzz. Could it mean eternal crisis? Live it up is the name of the play. It sounds like a very rock or ghetto show.

There was an old man standing at the entrance, he looked gray all over from his hair to his suit. He was passing out pamphlets.

"Nice." Celia complimented, as she smiled at the old man.

"I'm a pro," the old man said.

He must've made it himself.

There were many people taking their seats. We sat in the first row, which Syd always reserved for us. I sat in the corner, Celia sat in the middle, and Syd sat beside her.

This is going to be a very interesting show. In the pamphlet, it says the play will be involved with great music. I don't think it's going to be like a

Broadway musical. Most probably, EternalCryzz will perform music in some parts.

"I don't think that will happen in the end." Celia yelled at Syd. People's eyes were suddenly glued at her.

"Celia, quiet down! Hey, James told me that a little boy would die." His explanations have no sense of meaning sometimes.

"Huh?" They both lost me there. How can the boy die? That's not what it

says in the pamphlet. The play will spread with a stirring ending. The boy will

end up traveling around the world, meets his future wife in South America

and sacrifice will happen.

I felt these two were going get it on in the theater, like old folks, they usually argue about nothing. What a sneak preview. It's crazy to leave these two together, but unfortunately, kind Celia is taken. Here he goes again, trying to prove her that he's always right. She'll find a way to make him feel ugly. I don't even give any attention to his la, la ego. Celia is loud, but smart enough not to get into Syd's mind tricks.

I heard a loud giggling sound coming from the second row, behind where I am seated. A smirk appeared on my face. I'm just too curious to see who this person is. Was it really that entertaining?

"Lynna, hello? You want anything to drink?" Celia asked. "No, thanks." I replied.

"Ok! Syd get me a coffee," she said.

 "You're hyper enough." he said. "Just get me one."

Celia handed five dollars to him to get her the drink. "

Keep it, my treat." Syd offered.

"Oh, how nice, then get something for Lynna too."

"I really don't want anything." I said.

"It's on me." Syd said, as he got up.

"While he's doing that, I'll go to the ladies room. Lynna, you should stay here and look after our seats."

I nodded yes, but still too curious.

I had to turn around, but slowly pretending to see if the back seats were filled,

"Yep indeed." I said.

I quickly took a glimpse to see who had giggled. No one familiar, I thought. He gave me a friendly smile, with a warm "Hello."

I responded to his hello and noticed he's seated alone. There were two old women seated beside him. There is no way he is with them, unless it's his grandmothers. This person is dressed in a blue business suit. He has straight brown wet hair to match his brown eyes, and his light skin.

Where was this going to? Ah, yes.

"May I ask what you were giggling about?" nosy little me, I have to know.

I couldn't look into his eyes, while I was asking him the question. His face was so ravishing that it was hard to look at. I was looking somewhere else instead.

"Your friends like to fight huh?"

"Oh, that's the way they communicate."

"How long have they been together?"

"Together? Never. There are not together." That was a good one.

"Really?"

There was a long silence. I was watching the people coming in from the back entrance, and saw the old pamphlet man finally taking his seat.

I'm not that boring if you think. What else am I supposed to say? I just turned my head back in front of the stage.

I noticed Celia had already returned from the ladies room, sipping on her hot coffee and Syd drinking his orange soda.

Syd handed me a lemon lime soda. "Thanks" I said.

"I'm Scott." I heard, and turned my head back to him, "I'm Lynna."

The lights are dimming low and I just swirled back in the front. The audience are screaming loud, clapping, and whistling.

"I'm so ready to see this!" Celia said, with exciting intensions. She goes crazy for these types of motion shows. Soap operas came first though.

"Lynna, you have your cam with you?" she asked.

"Yeah, I do." I said.

Most of the time, it's in my handbag.

There could be moments one day where you need to still shoot it. I'll just take some pictures, when it's needed to.

This Scott guy introduced himself with a friendly gesture, or can it be more? He is certainly a gentleman with his politeness, or it could be from his suit, worn on a Saturday afternoon. I have a gutsy good feeling about it. He reminds me of a runaway model, in a suit.

The show has started.

Hello I said, I hope this isn't the end, with a smile I never showed to anyone, except you…

That poem was swirling in my head.

Let me get back to the play, James does look good. He's such a character.

His black hair reflected from the spotlights, and his brown green eyes were twinkling very mysteriously. I remember when he was just a kid, he had this thing with rock stars. He had a little wooden guitar, which his mom had bought him when he turned 11 years old. He invited me over at his place, sometimes my sister came along too, as a quick audience. He was a bit embarrassed to perform in front of his friends. The dining room table was his stage. He used to stand up on it, and do the most unusual moves, when his mom was not there of course. Perhaps, he still does that.

Every time when he returned home from his Saturday music class, he needed to show someone what he had learnt to play. He was too proud of himself.

"That guy is such a good guitar player, do you know him?" It was Scott's voice coming from the back. I turned my head to his direction again.

"Yes, I know him, that's James, a friend of mine." I replied.

I could say more than just a friend, starting with a neighbor, and then a crush for a while. We kissed at my parents' cottage on the summer before we had started our first year in high school. We did not spark until another summer had come, before our senior year. He asked me out on a couple of dates. It was a short progress, but what was special, he kept on reminding me on some good times we had together, by giving me cute handmade things. That's it, since that year. I'll never know what's been going through in his mind. He is not much of a talker, but he has been there for me all my life.

Scott didn't look very interested after, when I answered.

He looks at his watch to check the time.

"Hey, you want to go for coffee tonight?" he changed the subject, and continued, "If you don't have anything to do…Maybe you might have plans?"

I started to feel a pressure of air swirling around me, my heartbeat ran quickly. That's a sign.

I did daydream of him when the show had started.

"Sure, why not…" I answered. My heart could melt right now.

He took out a pen and a note pad from his business jacket pocket, and wrote something.

"Here's my number, just in case there is a change of plans."

"I should do the same." I said.

He handed me the pen and the note pad, and I wrote down my digits.

"Let's meet at seven o'clock in the coffee place, between Crescent and Saint Catherine Street," he suggested.

"Ok." I said.

I assumed it's the mini French café, he was going on about.

I turned back in front of the stage, watching James, and the other characters of the show.

Syd keeps on whistling every time a scene is done.

Even though I don't know this Scott, all I know that we have one thing in common, coming here and watching the show. That sounds corny, I know.

Hours flew by, and the show had ended.

While I was leaving my seat, and entering the aisle, Scott stopped in front of me, blocking my way.

"See you later," he said, as he gave me a quick look, and slowly walked to the exit door.

There was a traffic of people wanting to get out of the theater. I saw Scott turn around, he was looking my way. I gave him a quick good-bye wave.

I am a little nervous. I didn't have the strength to look into his eyes at that moment, but we will have a conversation once again tonight.

There were no sign of Syd and Celia. I knew they had gone to the dressing room to find James. He has to dress into his normal day clothes. He had a matching outfit like the rest the band to wear. I went to wait in the hallway.

The car was parked a mile away, which gave me the time to think about the odd feeling I'm getting.

On the way home in Syd's car, I was really quiet. Celia and I are seated in the back. James sat in front of me and Syd was driving. They are discussing about the show.

The play was traditional, the little boy sees how the family was raised, and then ends up marrying a girl. After the girl gives birth to a child, she gets sick and the guy had to work very hard to pay for their health care, well something like that. I didn't really pay any attention to it. You know me, when I don't listen, that defines I'm not really there.

Celia was waving her hand in front of my face.

"Earth to Lynna." she yelled.

Laughter rumbled.

I just had to whisper the news in her ear. "I have a date tonight. He's very good looking, and smart." Her eyes grew wide, and her giggles appeared loudly. I continued "I'll be seeing him tonight."

"Lynna, that's great!" she yelled.

"Damn, Celia, what's up with the screaming all the time?" Syd said, as he was getting annoyed by it.

"What's going on?" James asked. "Nothing." I said.

 "Celia, why are you acting like a jelly bean?" Syd asked. "Syd, this has nothing to do with you."

"Sorry Madam."

He laughed.

It feels like a long ride, I can't wait to get home, and get ready for this event.

"What are you guys doing tonight?" I said, as I changed the subject.

"James and I have plans, we are heading to the pool bar, and you and Celia can join us." Syd offered.

"Yeah, Lynna, I could show you some pointers." James suggested. "That would be great, but I will have to take a rain check on that." "Oh, ok, you're busy then?"

"Yes, sorry."

"Celia?"

"Oh no, I can't either." "Ah, your man."

"Yup."

"Man? That sucks!" Syd interfered.

"Syd, watch the road," she said.

That was weird, James did not even bother to ask why I will be busy. We reached in the area not far from Westmount.

Syd turned into my street and double parked.

"Alright guys." Syd said.

James and I got out from the car.

"Thanks for the ride." I said."

"No problem."

"We'll phone." Celia said from the back window. I nodded yes.

She's next to be dropped off, even though she lives ten seconds away from my place.

She has her lazy days.

The car speeded down the street.

"I'll see you around Lynna." James said, as he was walking towards his

place.

"Yeah, later."

While unlocking the door, I watched James walk away, with his hands in his pockets, and then I went in the house.

I went in my bedroom, grabbed my make up bag, and stood in front of the long vertical mirror. I just had some touch ups to do on my face. I was watching my brother Kyle, running back and forth with an action hero toy in his hand, making space-landing sounds at the meantime.

I guess I forgot to close my door, anyway, what's up with him?

I'm letting my crazy wavy red hair down tonight, I usually have in a tight ponytail. With school, and work involved in my life, it has become a tradition to have my hair up all the time.

"Must close the door now." I said to myself.

I wore my loopy gold earrings, my beige top with my black bell-bottom pants, and a black chocker.

"I'm going out now." I said to my parents, while passing the kitchen. They were seated at the table, and eating their supper.

"No supper?" mom asked.

"Nah, I'll get a bite to eat later." I said, while I was putting my shoes and jacket on.

"Bye." dad said.

"Later!"

I grabbed my handbag, and ran to the door.

It is almost six o'clock, I walked down on Sherbrooke Street to Victoria Avenue. There are plenty of strange people around at this time, so I have to speed it up to the subway.

I got off at Guy station, and walked down to Crescent. There was loud music erupting the streets, and vibrant lights, flashing from the discotheques long narrow windows. People are yelling, and cars speeding. There is life out here, all you can see are bars, gift stores, restaurants, disco clubs, and lounges. The Montreal nightlife, as they call it.

I'm passing by the entire craziness, watching people waiting in lineups to enter in a lounge, others are drinking inside the bars, and outside on the streets, with clouds of smoke surrounding in the fresh spring air. Finally, I arrived at the café. The place looks like a very tiny diner, with two floors. I went inside, sat at the nearest table, and waited for Scott to arrive.

"Lynna, I'm right here."

The voice sounded like Scott's. He was already sitting at the café's bar stand, near the entrance door. I went and sat beside him.

"I didn't see you sitting here." I said.

"Well, hello darling," he said. "I've been waiting for you for 10 minutes." He giggled with a silly face.

He is still wearing that business suit he wore this afternoon. He must've had no time to change.

"Oh, yes?" I said.

"How've you been, since, from the last couple of hours?" "Very good, how are you?" I had to ask.

"Great. We shall get some coffee, or any other kind of those hot drinks?" "Umm, ok. I will get a cappuccino." I had to decide rapidly.

"Fine, then I will have the same."

Scott called the waiter, and asked for two cappuccinos.

"You know, let's have an apple pie with it," he suggested.

It was fine with me, even though, he didn't ask if I liked it, or wanted any. The waiter wrote the order down, and left.

"Were you born here?" he asked. "Yes, you?"

"No, I'm from Oakland, California." "Why did you come here?"

"My parents got divorced when I was very little, and my mom had custody of me. We moved here, my grandmother lives here anyway."

The waiter brought our cappuccinos and apple pies.

"You never thought of going back?" I asked.

"Not really, I will someday, but I made most of my life here."

"Yeah."

"You go to school?"

"Yes and you?"

"Did, got my degree in business four years ago. I have opened a small company, we sell statues to clients for their offices and homes."

"That sounds interesting. I'm majoring in advertising."

"Wow! You're going to be working like those people who make ads?"

"Yeah," I said. "I also work part time at a home decorating store near Saint Catherine's street."

He just nodded as if he understood. It looked like it didn't impress him that much.

I really am enjoying this conversation.

Soon after that, there wasn't any cappuccino left in our cups, and the pie was delicious.

Scott pulled his wallet out from his jacket pocket, took some money, and

left it on the bar stand for the waiter.

We had our slight prologue today, but it seemed that we were more concentrated on our desserts.

"You live close by?" he asked.

"Sort of."

He looked at his watch and continued.

"Ok, I live around here, it's getting late, I'll give you a ride near your place."

We left the café.

His silver machine was parked on Mackay Street, all he had to do is drive up to Sherbrooke. It's ten to fifteen minutes away.

"You're a good girl." he complimented, as we were walking on the sidewalk.

"Thanks." I said.

"I mean it, you're so calm, and quiet." We went into his machine.

He was much of the talker. At every red traffic light we stopped to, he had something to say. I did feel that as though, I was on a tour. He pointed out at almost every building he saw, and described his merry events on Sherbrooke Street.

"You see that restaurant there?"

"Yes?" what is it this time?

"I made a fortune, I found customers instantly, while I was having Szechwan for lunch one day."

I could say good for you, or something else, but it really didn't wow me. "You found clients?"

"Yeah."

He did not explain how it happened. The traffic light turned green.

We came across near the duplex.

"There's my place." I said, as I pointed it out. "All right, I'll leave you here."

He doubled parked in the corner of the street.

"Thanks for the night." I said, while I unbuckled my seat belt.

"No, thank you." He leaned over, and gave me a kiss on the cheek. I opened the door and got up from the car.

"Good night." I whispered, while having a thought I would wake up everyone across town.

"Good night."

He saw me walk to my door, and drove.

My nerves were jumping with anticipation.

I rushed inside, passed the kitchen, and saw it was already past ten at night from the wall clock.

It was not really late, perhaps he wanted to make a first good impression taking me home early.

I ran upstairs to my bedroom, and quickly got undressed. I had one more thing to do before going to sleep. I took my yellow journal out, which was placed in between the two mattresses of my bed. I always liked the color yellow, it gave me a rich powerful feeling every time I wrote something.

Hello Journal,

It is a night of spring, and I just arrived home from a date. If you were human, you would say "Really? It has been a while Lynna."

Scott is the guy who I spent my three hours with. He looks very much upgraded, a businessperson, with a very sharp modelish sense of appearance. I was very quiet, and he just kept on talking.

Nite,

Lynna

SGW University

I skipped like a little girl to the University library on De Maisonneuve Street, the next morning.

I usually come here when there is an assignment to do, or meet up with Celia.

I had those moments, where utterly not really concentrating on what the teacher has been explaining, in advertising class. I did write notes, but didn't really pay attention what was going on in class. I have to catch up. Mr. Paddero had given us a booklet of papers the other day.

There is an assignment to be done, which is due really soon.

The teacher had given the students copies of storyboards, to come up with a creative commercial, with drawings, and a theory thesis.

My idea deals with beauty, a perfume commercial. It has to be very rational. I named the perfume, Fleur, no alcohol, just real fresh lilacs, and lilies.

A woman would be dreaming of herself running into a garden with petals, falling from the sky, like rain. She has flowers in her hair. Once she is awake from her dream, she sees petals filled on her bed. She grabs some in her hands, and throws them on top of her. Cute, but corny.

Celia is always at the library on Sundays. If she's not, she must have an important reason. She also has a part time job once a week at the pet store, she would smell like pet food after work. Her studies seem to be scheduled randomly, she does make time for other important tasks though.

I am bound to bump into her on the second floor in a corner, napping her head in her books. I got out of the elevator and saw Celia, not only with her books, but with her Antonio, her other responsibility. They are sitting in front of each other, face to face, talking, while the books were left open on the table. She met the guy a couple of years ago, before our senior year in high school, at a coffee place where they used to work.

They have inseparable moments, there was a time where they went on and off, because Antonio liked to travel and Celia couldn't. She always studied for school. Antonio was happy about that, he sees her as a hard worker. Antonio did his studies when he was working at the coffee place. It's when all the magic began. He finished a course in tourism, and now he's working at a travel agency.

I went over there.

"Hey, you guys, what's up?" I said in a quiet tone. "Lyn, how are you?" Antonio asked.

"Great, how about you?"

"Good."

 "I hope you are, since good things are sparkling with you." Celia said, with a goofy look.

"Yeah." I sat down and started to take my books out of my book bag.

"Good stuff huh?" Antonio looked curious.

"Yep."

"Well, I would want to know, but having a girl talk would be better off between you two."

“What brings you here Antonio?” I asked.

“Celia wanted to see me, I wanted to sleep and watch TV.” I giggled quietly.

“It’s too bad you didn’t come see the show yesterday, it was great.”

“I had to work. There was a customer that had last minute plans to travel. He called me to settle the input. Crazy man, he had to pick my day off, for his trip to Asia.” he paused for a couple of seconds, and continued, “I heard Syd was around driving Celia crazy.”

“Yeah, he had to be there.”

“I’m not a fan of his, you both know that.”

Antonio never liked Syd around Celia. Syd enjoyed getting into

Catastrophic scenes with her. He had a feeling Syd likes her.

Teasing is another old trick to hide emotions by a guy. Celia does not like it when he bothers her at all. Her loudness is a normal thing, she can’t help it. I think she needs to be careful while Mr. Antonio is in her life.

"Syd is just Syd." I said.

"Syd is just too exposed." he answered. We three got silent.

"Ok babe, I'm going to go, I'll see you later." Antonio got up, leaned over, and gave a kiss on her forehead.

"Where off to?" she asked.

"Home, and have a good rest." "Ok, bye, bye."

"Bye, guys."

"Bye." I said.

We watched Antonio walk to the elevator.

"So we shall hit the books?" Celia suggested. Our chatting continued.

"He seems mad." I said.

"Not mad, just upset. I feel though it's my fault, when I'm around Syd, I give in."

"You're being you, you just can't be mute because you're attached."

"Honestly, I should. Syd does get on my nerves a lot, I know he does it on purpose."

"Ok, well if I were you, act cool next time."

"Yeah, I will, but next time, I'll make sure Antonio is with me at every event."

"Ok."

"Like my brown platform boots?" Celia asked, while she lifted her right leg, to show one of them to me.

"They are real suede."

"Oh my!" I said sarcastically.

"Let's talk about you and that guy." She changed the subject.

"Scott."

"Yeah, I did see you come home last night."

"Were you spying?" we started to laugh.

"Lynna, I live near you, not even a minute away. I was in my bedroom studying, until Antonio came to pick me up around ten thirty. You know my desk is situated in front of the window."

"So, what did you see?" I was curious.

"First please tell me, did you have a good time?"

"Yeah."

"I saw a guy in a convertible, and you stepping out of it."

"What else?" I hoped she had something good to say.

"I noticed you got off in the corner."

"Yeah, he decided to drop me there."

"Why did he do that?"

"I don't know, he wanted to. You know, he's a business man."

"Really? What type of business does he do?"

"He sells statues to clients for their offices and homes."

"Ok, tell me more. You had mentioned that he is good looking and smart, so I really don't have much of a description there."

"He's very much independent with his decisions. He has straight brown wet hair, brown eyes, light skin…"

Celia laughed.

"Is he the pretty boy type?" "I don't know."

"You don't know? Just don't get your feelings too tingly yet, do what's right."

"Sure," I said.

We had quiet down. She studied and I was working on my assignment. The weekend had ended just like that.

I'm at Celia's, we are planning to head downtown at the mall. Celia is getting prepared, while I'm putting my shoes on. I can hear the nearest church bells ringing very loudly, as it is now six o'clock. She has to exchange a jacket she had bought last week. I decided to tag along with her, and get some fresh air on a Thursday evening.

Celia lived in a two bedroom apartment with her parents, and shared a room with her sister Carol lee. We called her Sara lee like the cake. I never heard such a name like that. Celia was lucky to have a better name. Carol lee was more like a snob, she had her own click. She was like a wolf, working night shifts, sleeping too little, and going out with her stuck up friends. She's rarely home. Carol lee organizes scary snob meetings of gossip. She loves hanging out on the rich side of the city.

We were walking over to Sherbrooke Street, the cold wind started to chill both our necks.

Celia had opened a conversation about taxes. Tax season is around the corner.

"I want to do peoples taxes this year." she said.

"Can you?"

"Yeah." I studied it last semester, did a practice." "Sure, then go ahead."

"It will be extra money. I'll charge them fifteen or twenty dollars." "Yeah, even that's expensive to do."

"Yeah."

There was a sweet smell in the air.

"Do you smell it?" I asked her.

"What?" Celia sniffed. "Yeah, it's, it's…"

"Shisha!"

"Oh." Celia's eyes opened wide.

The aroma of the hookah-shisha reminds us of the old man who lives in the apartment across her place. Every summer night, he sat down on his balcony floor, and took a puff of it.

"Old man puff." I said.

"Yeah, I wonder if he will be continuing his puffs this summer."

subway

We walked into the humid alley down the subway, and sat down on the bench as we waited for it to come. The place looks like a mess by the end of the day. It was dusty and dry, with all sorts of garbage lying around the floor.

The subway arrived, we went in and sat next to the right window. We were on the orange line, and had to get off once we arrived downtown.

We mellowed out by the movement of the wagon, speeding and stopping.

"What's that…?" Celia asked.

"What's what?"

"Do you smell that?"

"No."

There's a sudden reek of smell near our side, it was not shisha this time. "It smells like pee!"

Celia looked up and saw a man with dirty clothes and hair, passing by our way and walking towards the nearest subway door.

I started to smell it.

"Yeah!" I said.

Celia was covering her mouth with her blue scarf.

"Why would a dirty man smell like that? Does he have a home to wash up?"

"Never heard of a bathroom, I suppose." I said.

 "Oh, I don't like this smell…" Celia said, with a disgust look on her face.

The man was fixing his hair, while looking at himself, reflecting from the subway's window door.

His hands were charcoaled black, his white clothes were gray, and his hair was too oily.

The man finally got off to his stop. Celia felt like gagging.

"Why does he not take a shower?" she asked.
"Has no time." I said.

We were quiet until we walked to Ste Catherine Street, and I was following Celia wherever she had to go.

We arrived in the women's department at Simpson's, looking for the cashier.

An old woman perhaps in her sixties, was standing behind the cash register. She was spending her time putting returned receipts in a folder. She was tiny, had fuzzy gray hair, and dark blue eyeglasses.

"Hmmmm…Mrs.?" Celia said, to get her attention.

"Oui?" the woman as known as Colette, written on her nametag replied.

"I bought this jacket last week, I want to exchange it, or just get my money back."

"Bien sure," she said, which meant of course in French.

"Votre facture s'il vous plait." She continued, asking for the receipt. Celia gave it to her.

"Un reimbursement ok?" Celia quickly decided to have a refund.

The woman made a new receipt for her. After that, she took the jacket and placed it on the back counter of the cash register.

"Sign here please," the woman said.

Celia signed on one of the receipts.

"Your address and phone number too." she added.

So she did.

After that, we took a walk outside until we came to the nearest subway station to go home.

What an outing it was with Celia. We arrived in our area, and both went in

our different directions. I came home, heated some supper, and went to watch

TV.

 "I want to take you out for an early supper tomorrow."

Scott had called me in the middle of watching the bewitched show. I am interested in getting to know him more.

"Wear a nice casual dress, look good as every day. I will stroll down your street, and then we will have a good time."

"Oh, that's nice!" it's a fancy thing.

I didn't understand his schedule yet. I have a class the next day at eight to ten in the morning, and then I am free, so I'll be returning home early to get ready.

"How about work?" I said.

"Work is less tomorrow, Lynna is more."

I really didn't understand what he meant, but I liked what he said. I heard a coughing sound on the phone.

"You all right?" I asked.

"Yeah, fine, so I'll see you tomorrow at one." "Ok, good night."

"Night."

Like a little girl, I threw myself on my bed, and sighed.

"Forget about TV for tonight, I got a busy day to think of." I told myself. I slept with my day clothes on, silly me I was tired.

My Friday morning class was a drag to attend to. I had to wake up early, before the birds were awake, but as it was ten o'clock, I was free like the birds. Marketing class didn't want to go in my head today. It's a good thing there's one more class left before the finals. I'm probably not going to attend the last class, and start working on Fridays instead.

I'm at home, Hayley is still asleep, I know she has to work in the afternoon. I left my book bag in my room, took some things I needed, including my flowered pink dress for my second adventure of the day, and went to the bathroom, to take a nice bath, and get myself ready.

"I'll be done by the time Hayley gets up," I said to myself, as I rushed down the hallway.

"An hour must do."

I closed the bathroom door, put everything on the counter, and got the warm water ready.

I'm in the bathtub, lathering my hair with shampoo, and just started singing.

"Wooooooooooeeeeee, do you see?" I didn't know what I was singing "Hey! Yeah! What do you see?"

I left the shampoo in my hair, while I was washing my face with a cleanser. Corny, but you'll save time.

Corny seems to be one of my cool words to say.

When was Scott supposed to come get me? One o'clock yes, yes. If he does call while I'm in here, it's going to wake Hayley up and that's not going to be good. She'll growl like a lion.

I rinsed my hair, and got out of the bathtub. Quickly wore my dress, and ran out of the bathroom to my bedroom, with a whoosh of wind.

Hayley was not there. I quickly fixed my wet hair with gel, to make it look all funky, and wore some perfume, earrings, sandals, and panties to keep warm. I took my mini black purse, and put extra money in it.

The phone rang.

"Hello?"

"Hi, it's me Scott." good, he just called.

"Hey." I said, as I was running around in my room to see where I had put my lipstick.

"How's it going?"

"Good, you?"

"Good, I'll be there very soon. I expect you to be outside."

"Ok."

"Bye."

That felt like a dry conversation, but so what, I'm going to go outside, and wait for him.

I went downstairs towards the hallway closet, where my long black jacket was hanging. I heard Hayley munching on something in the kitchen, while I was putting it on.

"I'm going out!" I yelled, so she can hear me. "Uh where?"

"Out."

"Ok?" she said, with an unusual voice.

"Yeah, see you later." I said, and ran to the door. "Yeah, later."

I didn't even tell my own sister what was happening in my life. She would have many questions to ask, if she knew. I will tell her eventually.

I just had a "sigh" moment like in the novels.

I arrived to the corner of my street, standing there, under the sun, waiting for my ride. I suddenly got nervous.

Scott drove by some minutes later. I went in his silver machine, and gave him a peck on the cheek.

"We're going to go somewhere far today. Enjoy this ride."

"Where are we going?"

"You will see."

He turned on the radio, and found a station, which he liked, a weird disco song was playing.

"You like surfing?" he asked.

We're going surfing with this dress? I thought. "I never surfed."

"It's great. You've been at the beach?"

"Yeah."

"Some friends and I are planning to go this summer. It will be good. Take some time off."

He sounds happy about it.

"That's good." I said.

"Any plans this summer?"

"Work, go out with friends. I don't think I'll be going on vacation." "

Ok, well I am."

I giggled at his sarcasm.

We drove across the highway. I was paying attention of where we were going.

Moments later, we came up to a lake. The coldness entered from the machine's windows. Scott made a right turn and found an empty spot to park.

He stopped, and told me to get out of the car.

"Something wrong?" I asked.

"No, this is where I'm taking you."

We both got out of the car, and he started to walk towards the pier. I was behind, following him.

"I like this view, what do you think?" he asked.

The view is a lake. You can see the other side of Montreal. There's a bridge on your far left, it takes you there.

"It's nice." I said.

 "It's enhanced."

"Ok."

"You know Lynna, I come here when I need to. "Any reason?"

"My problems will float away for a while. It's a good break." "It is." I said.

There were a couple of big rocks around. Scott sat on one of them. I was still standing.

"Sit." he said.

It was a bit cold on a mild April afternoon, I made sure my long black jacket was on the rock, so I could sit on it to keep warm.

"Do you smoke?" he asked.

"No, you?"

"Yeah, but I forgot my pack at home." He came closer to my side.

"Come, don't be afraid."

I came closer to him, and he put his arm around me.

"What are your plans after graduation?" he asked.

"Work."

"Advertising?"

"Yes."

"I don't think there are many jobs in that field here."

I thought he was excited about it, when I told him what I was majoring in, while we were at the café on our first date.

"Yes, there are."

"Whatever."

We did not have much to say after that.

We returned back to the car before it got dark. "This is what I wanted you to see."

I was looking at the yellow sun, setting. Scott reached my right shoulder with his hand, and kissed me. He was holding me tight. Suddenly he stopped.

"Lynna, your mine." he said, and then continued to kiss me. I had a big gushy smile on my face. I felt my cheeks turning red.

After that, he took me somewhere for supper. It was a little bistro place.

He ordered a fruit smoothie for both of us, with whipped cream on top.

"You have a nice complexion on your face tonight." he complimented.

"Thanks." I didn't say it's because of all the smooching that made me go red.

"How's your drink?"

"Interesting."

"You're supposed to say refreshing babe." "Yes it is…"

"New stuff huh?"

"Yeah."

I was using a spoon to eat the whipped cream, and then drank the smoothie with a straw.

"How's work?" I asked.

"Good, always plenty of things to do." "How's your schedule?"

"Busy."

"Do you work on working hours?" Dumb question, but I needed a normal answer.

"Twenty four hours a day are my working hours." "When do you work?"

"I just told you, I'm the boss there."

"Ok."

I guess he worked when it was busy there. "Are you ready to eat?"

"Isn't this already enough?"

The smoothie made me full.

"No, this is just a little drink. How about, you get a meat platter?" he suggested.

"I really am not into meat." I said.

"You will be, once you see what I will order for you,"

He was looking through the menu, and then continued.

"Here's a nice kebab platter with vegetables, and rice. That's sounds nice." I didn't want it, but he ordered it anyway.

Our drinks on the side were water, and his plate was pork.

I slowly ate the rice and the vegetables, and cautiously stared at the kebabs. "You want some of my kebabs?" he asked.

Not only I had my own, there would be no way I would eat his. "No, thanks."

After watching Scott eat his whole plate, we stepped out of the place, and went back to his car.

It was nearly nine o'clock.

I was sitting there, waiting for him to move his silver machine, but he didn't, instead he looked at me.

"I will take you home soon."

"You have plans?" I wanted to know what he was up to later. "Yeah. I'm going to visit my grandmother."

"She lives far from here?"

"More to the west."

That's nice I thought, but doesn't his grandma sleep at this time?

He came closer to me, and stared into my eyes. Plainly kissed my left cheek, and went back to his seat.

He turned on the ignition.

"We need some heat in here," he said.

"Yes."

He turned on the heater and the radio.

The disco music was amusing until the way home.

That was that, I got undressed, and wore my pajamas. He didn't call that night. I was curious to know how the visit went with his grandma.

Journal,

I will remember this night, a moment where no one can take it from me.

Lynna

Montreal Canada

The days go by fast when you have plans, or when all I could think of is Scott. He took me places, which I haven't been for awhile. The way he expresses his thoughts, and the way he thinks is incredible. Lynna is in la la land. My heart was heavier than ever.

Tuesday afternoon had come, my art history class just finished. Before going to the subway, I went to a corner payphone, and called him.

"Hello?"

The voice didn't sound like Scott's. "Hi, is Scott there?"

"Nope. Are you…? I forgot your name."

"Lynna."

"Yeah, I guess. I'm his roommate, he went to work, he'll be back later."

"Ok, ok. Thanks bye." I was about to close the phone, but heard him continue talking.

"He's looking for you."

"I see."

Interesting.

"He had mentioned something about going around your area to see you because, he misses you…"

"Oh, thanks."

"Yeah, bye."

"Bye."

I got anxious.

He misses me? I'll call him again, as soon as I get home! I thought.

"Forget about the subway!" I said to myself, "I'll run to Sherbrooke, and take the bus from there. It's quicker to get home!"

I finally arrived home, huffing and puffing, with a shortness of breath. I called him.

"Hello?" he said. He's home. "Hey!" I said.

"Hi?" It sounded like he wasn't sure who it was. "It's Lynna."

"Hey, how are you?" he said with a flirty voice. "Good, what are you up to?"

 "Nothing, I just arrived home. Babe, let's meet somewhere." "Ok, where?"

"Stay where you are, I'll find you." "I'm at my place."

"Ok, I'll be there shortly."

I heard sounds from the background.

"What are you doing?" I asked.

"That's not important, later."

He hung up the phone.

It was only two in the afternoon, working hours I thought would he be missing it? What's not important? I'm getting confused.

I guess I just have to sit, and wait for him.

The phone rang, it woke me up from my daydream. I picked up. "Hello?" I said.

"Hey, it's Celia."

"What's up?"

"I'm calling from school, I'm going to go to my last class for today, you want to come over to my place, later?"

"Can't, he's picking me up very shortly."

"Really? So when am I going to meet this guy?" "I don't know, I'll let you know."

"He's not busy selling statues?"

"You know, he was at home, and I heard sounds from the background. I asked him, what was he doing, he said, it's not important, and hung up the phone."

"What? Lynna, ask him again. What's not important? Maybe it was, but didn't want to tell you."

"I'm not going to worry about nothing. Probably he was watching TV."

"Maybe, all right, Bye."

"Bye."

I started to get ready. I left a note on the kitchen table for my parents, telling them I won't be home until tonight.

Minutes later Scott's silver machine appeared on my street. I walked over, and went in the car.

 "Hey." he said, and gave me a kiss.

He started to drive in the downtown direction. The car had a very loud sound, when he speeded.

"Where are we going?" I asked. "To the movies."

"Really…I'm not in the mood to see a movie."

"There is a great suspense movie I would like to see." "I'm not very much into suspense." I said.

"You will like this one. It's cool. After a hard days work, suspense is the key."

I had no idea what was going on. So, he finished work for today?

We arrived at the movie theater, he bought the tickets, and then we walked to the snack bar.

"Hungry?" he asked.

"A little, I will get myself a popcorn, and a drink."

"Let's get a big bag for both of us." he suggested

"Sure," he paid, and then we went to sit in the theater. We are seated to watch an apprehensive movie.

The popcorn tastes like a shoebox.

"Babe, you like my new shirt?" The shirt is burgundy.

"Yeah, it's nice."

"Nice? I paid a hundred dollars for it at Hudson's The Bay!" "Why so expensive?" I asked.

"Why not? It brought to my attention."

He caressed my face with his hand, I was staring at his eyes, to look what he will do next.

He came closer to kiss me.

I closed my eyes and only heard sounds of Scott enjoying the moment.

We had to stop smooching soon after the movie started

I was not fascinated with the movie.

I took a little nap, while everyone in the theater was enjoying the entertainment.

Next thing you know, I'm dropped off at the corner, to walk home.

It's the following morning, I have class later in the afternoon. I'm sitting at the living room table, and reading over my daytime planner, just checking the events for the upcoming weeks. I had written homework for every day, and work once or twice a week. This Saturday is James' show, and I had circled it. I was too much in another world to think of it.

"There's lunch in the oven, if you are hungry." mom said.

"Ok." I replied.

"Well then, I'm off to work."

"Bye, mom."

"Bye."

The place was all to myself.

I'm going to call Scott, who knows if he was at work, but I also knew he would be glad to hear from me.

I dialed his number.

"Hello?"

"Hey, it's Lynna."

"Oh, hey…What's up?"

"Nothing really. I want to say thanks for the movie." "No problem, I assume you hated it?"

"It was interesting."

"Oh?" He chuckled.

I had just remembered what Celia had mentioned.

"Scott?"

"Yep?"

"Would you want to meet my friends?"

"Uh, sure."

"My friend Celia wants to meet you."

"I mean if I'm not busy…"

"Yeah."

"Lynna, excuse me, but I'm going to go now." "Ok, have a good day."

"Yeah, thanks."

He cut me off.

I went to the kitchen to heat my early lunch. While it's getting heated, I will continue working on my advertising assignment, which I will finally hand in today. Since I completed most of my homework earlier, I think I would have some time to spare to see Hayley. I rarely see her, either she is at work, or with her man David. It's been serious with him lately. They've known each other for a while, since their last year in elementary, but they started dating in high school.

I ate the baked potato and chicken, got dressed, and headed downtown.

The stores have been starting to look more colorful than ever. They were displayed with summer items.

Hayley works at Eaton's, in the women's department. As a future fashion designer, she spends hours looking at the new styles. She gets some ideas, and sketches them down, and then when she is home, she makes them. I know her duty is to do more than that, once she's a pro.

I took the escalator and went up to the third floor. Hayley was folding winter sweaters back in the boxes.

"Boo!" I said.

"Don't do that! Yes, you scared me. What are you doing here?" she said excitedly.

She was frightened.

"I have a class soon, but before that, I wanted to see you."

"Oh?"

"I haven't seen you lately, you're busy."

"Well yes I am, but is there a reason you're here?"

"No, really, I don't always come see you for every problem I have." I lied.

When we were younger, our seminars were in our bedroom. We had discussions about anything. Now, there's not much time to do these things. She's the type of sister that would not tell anything to anyone. It's a good thing for that, but she does have other sister characters that bug the heck out of me.

The only way she would know what's going on in my head is if she got it off of me.

"You have a break?" I asked.

"I can take one soon. You want to talk about something?"

"Maybe."

It's already one o'clock in the afternoon, I went out of her department, and found a payphone near by. While I wait for Hayley, I'll call Scott.

There is no answer.

Hayley came rushing.

There was a bench to sit next to the payphone. We sat down.

"Lynna, what's up?"

"School. The usual."

"When do you work?"

"Tomorrow."

"I'm working too, until when?"

"My shift finishes at five."

"Yeah? Same, but I'm going to meet up with David later." I changed the subject.

"How are you two doing together?" "Great. Why?"

"Just asking."

"Is something bothering you?" "I don't know."

"Tell me."

I had to say it.

"I'm going out with someone for about three weeks." "You kept a secret from moi?"

"I was going to say it sooner or later." "Ah, I already knew it."

"How?"

"I accidentally looked into your journal."

"What? So your hands, got stuck in between my two mattresses somehow, huh?"

We had to laugh. It sounded really sick, but funny at the same time.

It was actually ok for her to read my journal. I didn't write about very private things, only my day by day thoughts. She is a nosy one.

"What's the problem?" She asked.

"This guy is a good person. Everything a girl wants in the materialistic way, if you are one of them. He is attractive, funny. He has his own business and wears a suit."

Hayley giggled at the suit part. What's up with everyone doing that? Is a suit, a crime worn?

"Are you going out with someone way older than you are?"

"I think he is about four years older than I am, because he had mentioned he graduated University four years ago."

"Yeah, but that does not mean he could've been the same age as you, when he graduated."

"You're right."

"You know, if you're with someone way older, things can be like a see saw."

"How?"

"From your likes and dislikes, the age difference can be a big collision. You think university and he thinks business suits."

"Oh, yeah?"

"His character can be old too, the only way you guys might get along very well, is if you think the same, that's a different story."

"We get along, but my question is, why pick a young chick?"

"Because you are attractive, and you're full of potential. You can also be too nice, that can be a theory to take charge of everything. Girls his age have experience, and are very independent. You get my point here?”

Hayley was right, he just does whatever he wants without asking my opinions.

“You like him a lot?” she asked.

“I don’t know. It’s not even a month I’ve been with him, and I haven’t seen anything clear yet.”

“Let me give you an example, let’s say you went out with someone your age…”

“No, not with a kid.”

“Hey, David and I are nearly the same age, so let me finish.”

“Ok.”

“Let’s say James, he’s your age, and I see he is in your level. What I mean is that, he goes to school, he has skills, and potential. Yeah, he is in his own world at times, but so are you.”

“So, what’s your point?”

“You’ll get along better, and always have. And one last thing before I go back to work, some guys brains are clouded, they can’t express the way they feel, so there can be times where they don’t even bother saying anything at all. Especially someone who loves you."

I think she is trying to tell me something, but I ignored it. I know it's a hint.

"Well, no guy I know is hiding anything from me." I said something indifferently.

"No guy? What's his name?"

"Scott."

"This Scott guy is definitely hiding something from you, and it's not his suit!"

"What?"

"The truth, you are seeing the outside. Anyways, I know this is all bla, bla to you, give yourself time to think what you want in a person. If you feel uncomfortable with this one, you know what to do."

She is making sense with the Scott thing. It triggered me when he didn't want to say what he was doing at home, before he came to pick me up at my place that day. Nothing important. What's that supposed to mean?

"Is he really a gentleman? What did it, that made you feel good?" Hayley was questioning me.

"He takes me out, we mingle."

"Did he hold your hand yet? Drove you in front of the house, and waited there until you went in your home safely?"

"Is that important?"

"Yes. His actions play a role, and that clears his character." "How would I know, if what you are saying is true?"

"I'm letting you be aware. If you see that something you don't like is happening. You just have to stop it."

She was going on, and on about it. Why don't I notice these things? Hayley likes the traditional way, when a guy has to take her home, or whatsoever. I'm not saying she depends on her man most of the time, I guess if someone is independent enough to do things on their on, they don't consider thinking about these things. But everyone has its choice. If you feel alright with the fact to be self sufficient, then it's fine.

"Lynna, that's all I've got to say for now. My break is over. I'll see you later."

"Ok, thanks." We both stood up, she gave me a hug, and drifted off, back to her department.

I took my direction to the escalator.

Am I ever clueless of life? How did Hayley know what to answer so fast? I had to speak out with a proficient. Who needs a counselor when you have people like her to talk to?

I was a bit confused. Sometimes it's hard to believe what people can tell you until you see it with your very own eyes.

Journal,

I lie on my bed and think of him. Is it clear to see with whom I am with?

Two days had past, I was seated at the kitchen table that morning, nibbling on my breakfast, toasted bread with strawberry jam. Celia had come over.

She's also having breakfast, slurping on her last drops of milk from the bowl of cereal, while reading the newspaper. I kept on staring at the blue round clock on the wall.

"You alright?" she asked curiously. "Yeah, perfect." I lied.

"You are acting very strangely. You ok?" "Umm…Yes."

I wasn't talking, there was a silence for a bit, until Celia started talking again.

"James has the show Saturday night, we're going to have a big party for the opening of Syd's new theater!"

She said it as though we're going to a new year's bash. "That's nice." I said.

Suddenly my stomach turned upside down, and I wasn't feeling good anymore.

"Oh, no!" I yelled.

"What? What?" Celia looked scared.

 "James!"

He's in my stomach twirling, while Scott is pinching my soft sides.

He was completely off my mind all this time while seeing Scott.

"I'm really confused Celia, Scott hasn't called me for a couple of days." "Why not?"

"I don't know, I called him two days ago in the morning, he cut me off, and in the afternoon, there was no answer."

"That sucks, and it's not normal. He should've called you." "Yeah, he sounded very busy."

"Hmm…strange. By the way, did you ask him if he wants to meet me?" "Yeah, I did mention it."

"YEAH AND?" she said it too loud and anxiously. "He said sure, when he is not busy."

Celia looked at me with disgust in her face.

"This guy is hiding something." She got very angry, and continued. "I say forget about him!"

"I can't just do that."

"Yeah, you can. What, is he going to cry? Come on!" "Listen, he took me out, we smooched…"

"He left you at the corner, he didn't want to say what he was doing that day, before he came to pick you up…Did he even let your opinions spread?"

"I was fine with his decisions."

"You know, there is a saying."

"Huh?" I said.

"You are so in love, I think more infatuated with this guy, that you don't even see the truth of this person. Only people around you see it."

"I am, I am starting to."

"I don't know what's happening in your mind. I don't know what Scott is up to, and what about James?"

"My sister gave me a nice conversation about the difference between them. I think she was trying to tell me that some guys like James would connect with me better, then someone older."

"Older! Jeez, Lynna, how old is this Scott? Thirty?"

"Businessman in a suit, graduated four years ago…What would you think?"

"He's a player! Don't go further with this guy, he's probably seeing other girls when you're not around. Listen, I'm talking like this because you are my best friend, and I don't want you to get hurt, I want the best for you."

I started to feel nauseated and uncomfortable. However, I'm feeling less confused by getting some facts straight. I got a hello! Wake up call. All this time, I wasted it with flirtatious instability.

"Hello? You there?" Celia said.

"Yes." I took the last bite of my toast.

"I know James is suddenly in the picture. You know what to do with

Scott."

"Is this a test?" I asked. "A test for life."

"Am I ignoring something?"

"Yeah, the consequences. You're in a state, where everything is tied up right now."

I got her point.

"Any doubts?" she continued.

"Yes."

"Remember, choose wise."

I got up, and went to the kitchen counter.

"You've known James almost your whole life, you must know him well by now."

"Yeah, feelings are coming and going. He doesn't even know what's happening in my head, since we were sort of together."

Celia got up, took her bowl and spoon, and put it in the sink.

I got emotional.

"There is no reason to cry." she walked beside me, and gave me a hug.

My tears were dripping on my cheeks. I grabbed a paper towel from the counter, and dried them.

"What am I going to do now?" I said.

"What you think is right."

"I'll think about it today during work. It's such a hard decision. The only way to get my correct response, is to ask James personally, if he still woes for me. If not, I'll just get on with my life.

"I think it's going to be easy to break up with this guy." she said.

Celia was blunt about it. She already knew what was going to happen, if I continued staying with Scott.

If she and Hayley never chit chatted with me, I wouldn't know anything.

"You should call James and that guy." Celia suggested.

Celia took her handbag, hanging from the chair, and wore her navy-blue jacket.

 "I'm going to go home, there is plenty of homework to do. I don't have time on the weekend. I have to work at the pet store, and there's the event."

We went to the front entrance, and she opened the door.

"Bye." she said.

"Bye."

Minutes later, I grabbed my book bag, and headed off to work.

Sherbrooke Street

After a long-crowded bus ride to the end of Sherbrooke, I arrived at the deco store.

The day is blooming to a bright spring, we had many cloudy days of rain, finally there is a bit of sun today. In Montreal, spring is like freedom. Our winters tend to stay with us for a while. The weather can be so cold, and painful, like a freezing sunburn. The pain dissolves once you rise up the heater. It takes twenty minutes to feel normal again.

I arrived at the store, and went to the stockroom in the back, took off my jacket, and put my book bag on the floor.

There are many things that must be done. The morning will be ending quickly, with all the inventory paper work, once the manager distributes it in my hands. We have to send some items to another store branch. The lamps we'll be shipping look very artsy. They are brown, with tangerine colored beads flowing down, on the red lampshades. I have to do this work today, while other employees take care of the clients, and the unpacking of the new products. It's always a rotation.

I have to do something about James and Scott.

I have a perfect idea, I have a break in twenty minutes, I'll call James, and ask him if he can meet me here at the near by burger place, on my lunch break.

He's probably with Syd.

I finished packing the boxes, and left them in front of the stockroom door. I took my things, and headed in front.

"Teek, I'm going on my break." I said, while he was standing in front of the cash register.

"Ok." he said.

Teek's the manager, an easygoing middle-aged man, who dresses like a fashion guru. He has crazy blond streaks, which he had done himself in his gray hair. He is tall and medium build.

I walked around outside, and found a payphone. I dialed his number.

"Hel-lo?"

"Hi, it's Lynna."

"Oh, hey, what's up?"

"Not much, I'm working today, and I'm on my break now. How about you?"

"Oh, all right, I'm getting ready to go to the theater. Syd will pass by soon."

So, he was not around yet.

"James, can you do me a favor?" "It depends on what it is."

 "Can you meet me at the burger place, near where I work, at two?"

"Why?"

"I need to talk to you, it's very important." "Can we talk it over on the phone tonight?" "No, it really can't wait."

"All right, all right. But Syd's going to tag along. I'll put him somewhere where he won't interfere."

"Good."

"Well um…I'm going to continue getting ready." "Yeah, thanks."

"Cool, bye."

That worked pretty smoothly. I had a feeling of relief. I returned to the store.

The shipping is done, and now, I just have some boxes to open, and display the new products around the place. Beige is the trend color to work on for today. What I have to do is use the vanilla-scented candles from the boxes, and place them on the beige painted table. Every corner has a different color, and the same color of items have to be matched. Color coordination as they call it. Customers won't have to over think about what goes well with their whatever.

Occupied by this workout, lunchtime already had come quickly. I took my book bag with my belongings, and headed over to the burger place.

This place has always been busy at this time, until late evening. You had to wait at very dull long lines. I went to the shortest one. I bought some fries with a side of water.

I finally found an empty two-chaired table. I was munching on my fries, while waiting for James to arrive.

I took my daytime planner out of my book bag, and started to check when are the finals coming up. My last exam is on the first of May. That meant by next week, my social life will be cut down. After that, I would want to work more hours.

Perhaps, find something part time in my field too.

"Practice equals experience," my marketing teacher says. That's all I remember in that class.

I stopped writing, actually scribbling of nothing, and put my planner back into my book bag.

I saw James from the far, he spotted me sitting in the corner, he waved as he walked closer.

"Hi." I said.

"Hey, I can't stay too long, Syd's waiting for me." he said, as he sat down. "Where is he?"

"Around the streets. Hope he won't get lost." he said sarcastically. "Ok." I giggled.

It is time to say what is needed to. No how are yous, just get to the point,

Lynna.

"Umm, this will sound something out of the ordinary."

He was looking into my eyes so carefully.

"Have I crossed your mind lately?" I asked.

"Yeah."

I wanted to scream, but instead I started shaking my right leg. I'm nervous. I want more details.

"I meant more than the usual." I said.

I made him stare at me with curiosity, and waited for his response.

The silence had spread, until I heard a "hi" behind me.

I turned my head around, and realized James was staring at Scott all along. "Hi" James replied.

I gave an awkward smile.

Jeez! So, the silence was not about my question. Let's just think it was about that. I assumed he saw a ghost, because I felt I did so. Why is he here?

Why? Why I say?

"James, this is Scott." I had to do something.

Scott shook his hand,

the only thing he had to say is "Oh, the entertainer."

James did not seem to be bothered with his bla. He just cleared his throat.

"Where were we?" he said.

"Am I interfering?" Scott asked.

Was he!

"Yeah." James answered directly.

"James, just come with me for a second." I said. I got up, and grabbed my book bag.

James got up too.

"I'll be back, Scott." I said, but felt like not returning.

I left the dry fries, and the empty water container lay there on the table,

with him.

James and I started to walk fast, closely to the door.

We stopped, and sat on a bench outside.

"I'm going to ask you again, have I ever crossed your mind, more than a friendly feeling?"

James' eyes are sparkling and he said, "Are we in our teen moments again?" He took a deep breath, and continued. "I do think of you, time to time, never did nothing for it. After that last summer we had, I didn't even bother asking you about us, because all this time I was thinking, you probably forgot about these memories we both had together."

He gave a good talk there, it was cute, and I was smiling over it.

"I never did forget," I said.

"My worry was that, you forgot about them." then I blurted "I am sort of with Scott now, I won't get on with my life untl am sure…"

I had to open the Scott subject

The get on with my life, is a given sign he should understand. It's a way to wake him up, and see what's really going on.

"Hmmm, Scott? Does he have the hoots for you?" Absolutely a form of tease there.

I made a funny face.

He laughed.

He got the point.

"I'm sure you must've heard about me and him." I said.

"No, but I felt that this guy is somewhat in your life."

"Who told you?" I became nervous again.

"No one, I saw it with my very own eyes."

"How?"

"While I was performing at the play, you were seated in front of me, and I saw you talking to him."

Now that's something I never thought of.

"I guess Syd never knew about it, or else he would've had mentioned it to you."

"Yep."

I don't really recall what was going around me, when I had the conversation with Scott that afternoon. I was in a big cloud for two.

I know James is honest. He says what he knows, that is if you open his mind.

"You like that guy?" he asked.

"No."

"What changed?"

"Many things that I did not even notice. He was a nice guy, but more or less, things can happen."

"I see,"

Now what? I thought.

"This got me thinking more about you." He continued.

"What?" I said, for him to repeat those gushy words.

"This got me thinking more about you."

I like that.

"James we need to be serious from now on, we're not kids anymore, and if you are willing to put your heart with mine, than that would be great."

He smiled.

"Are you coming to my show on Saturday?" he changed the subject.

"Yes."

He smiled and said "I got to go, I'll see you later."

We both stood up, and he gave me a quick hug.

"Syd is wondering where I've been," he said.

"Yeah, we need to discuss more about this soon."

"Sure, bye."

"Bye."

I really wanted to continue the talk, but he had to leave.

The form of his figure decreased, as he walked further down the street.

I opened my book bag to look for my watch, I know it was thrown somewhere in there. I found it, and saw I only have four minutes left before my lunch break ends.

"Darn, Scott!" I said.

I went back to the burger place.

He looked happy, what was going on in his skull?

I felt very annoyed, he hasn't called me for days, and when he feels like it, he shows up, as if nothing happened.

"Hi." he said.

Yeah, yeah…What do you want? I wanted to say that. "That was James, the entertainer, right?"

He already knew that.

"Yes." I said.

This is cold.

"Nice guy."

"Yeah."

"How's my girl doing?"

 "Fine, what made you come here?" "I wanted to see you."

"Scott, you haven't called me in days."

"I was busy, what's with your mood today?"

"What!" I was starting to get angry.

"Relax, there's nothing. I had errands to do. I don't need to tell you everything."

"No, but some things you should. Maybe we're just hanging, are we dating?"

"Dating…"

"Dating? You think so, with whom?" I was so eager to get his response. "With you."

"Date when you want, when you have the time." "Nah, you're my girl."

"This conversation has no purpose." And I stopped talking there.

Do I have to yell, to make him understand he's crazy?

He looked at his watch, and then stood up.

"I better get going." he muttered.

I stood up too.

"What for another errand? Perhaps a date." I mumbled. He came closer to me, and gave me a cold hug.

"I'll call you around six o'clock."

Hey weirdo, I might be going out somewhere to have fun, thought about asking if I am busy? Not really.

"Ok." I said.

He went to the direction where the deco store is situated. I was walking very slowly, to get there myself.

I was ten minutes late, guru didn't make a fuss.

My shift finished at five o'clock. I took the bus home. I sat on the first seat of the right hand corner, while trying to ignore the problem. I was watching the scenery from the window. It's a great time to listen to music, where is the radio when I need one? I heard this thing called the Walkman will be invented one day, so that we can bring our cassette tapes, full of music with us, wherever we go.

I'm anticipated on that.

I arrived home, and saw my mother cooking supper in the kitchen. It seemed quiet, I guess nobody is home.

"Lynna, come to the kitchen!" She yelled, as she spotted me walking to the entrance hallway.

I left my book bag on the floor, my jean jacket on the hanger and headed to the kitchen.

"Yeah, mom."

"There is a special delivery for you." "Really? What is it?"

She pointed at a planter with blue begonias, that was placed on the wide kitchen counter.

I ran to it and checked who is it from. The first person that crossed my mind is James. But it was from Scott, the note said can't wait to see you tonight.

What tonight? Did we have plans? I could say oh we're going out tonight? I can't figure out what's in his brain.

"Who is it from?" mom asked.

"A person." I replied.

While she was mashing the potatoes, she looked at me and said

"You are not thrilled over flowers from a man?"

"Mom, it's not that I am not thrilled, this man is just a mystery."

"A mysterious man, interesting."

"Not the type where he's a hopeless romantic, with lighted candles."

"Oh, then?"

"Think opposite. Anyway you need help on something before I go to my bedroom and freak out?"

"No, it's fine."

"Ok."

I brought it up to my bedroom and put it on my dresser.

I called Celia at home, luckily she picked up. "Yes, it's me." I said.

"How was work?"

"Work was great, but not all the time."

"Huh? Did you do anything about James?"

"Yeah, I told him to meet me on my lunch break. Guess who shows up?"

"Scott, right?"

"Yeah, what a coincidence…Probably driving around the street that moment, and spying to see where I am."

"So what happened?"

"I was about to tell James everything I wanted to say, and then he came along. I made him wait for me at the table in the burger place, and took a walk with James. We had to sit somewhere else to talk. Everything is fine with us, but there are still things to discuss."

"Good, so that settled, and how about Mr. Business suit?"

"After the talk, James had to leave. I went back to my seat, and spoke about nothing with him. I told him off…"

"And?"

"He said he was busy with errands."

"What crap!"

"He cut the conversation short, and said he'll call me at six tonight."

"I see."

"Yep."

"So you didn't break it with him."

"Nope."

"Well, when he calls, just say it, and get it off your mind."

"Yeah, but get this, when I arrived home, I saw that, he had sent me blue begonias with a note, that said, can't wait to see you tonight."

"Ha, Ha! That's funny. Maybe it went to the wrong address."

"Hey, you're making me feel bad."

"You deserve better, wake up."

"Yeah, I'm awake," I took a deep breath, and continued

"Is Antonio coming to the show with you tomorrow?"

"Yeah, I'm happy. We're going to have a good a time Lynna, you'll see, you're going be relieved!"

"What if I break his heart? He really likes me."

"You know, we'll see if he does get hurt, or just leaves it be."

"Yeah, did you get any studying done today?"

"Yes, plenty, finals are coming up."

"I know! I won't even have the time to talk to you about nonsense!"

"Yup, yup!"

"We'll talk later. Bye"

"Bye."

The phone rang after that, and I quickly picked up. I looked at my clock, it was not even six yet.

"Hello?"

"It's Scott."

"Well, hello…"

"I know it's not six yet, but I was too anxious to know if you have received the blue begonias?"

"Yes, thanks."

"You ready to go?"

 "No, where?"

"Dear, I left a message with it,

 it was a hint, don't you get it?"

"Scott, I'm busy tonight." such a good excuse.

"You never told me."

"You never called back until today."

"What?"

That's it, say what?

"I can make my own decisions." I added.

"Yeah."

"You always make plans for us."

"Yeah so?"

"How about what I want?"

"Have what you want, now I'm going to be near your place soon."

"You don't get it, I said I am busy, and if you want to be honest with me, tell me why you stopped calling me, and suddenly came to see me at the burger place?"

Does he spy on me, on his television set?

"What's wrong with you? Your jibber jabbering has no sense," he said.

"No, what's wrong with you? You're playing with me."

"Nah, you're just too little to understand these things."

I got really silent, I couldn't continue talking. He made me feel like a child.

"Why so silent Lynna?"

"I don't think this is going to work out."

"Oh yeah?"

"You are a very one sided person."

 "Ha, ha! Relax babe." What a joke.

"Lynna, you're being silly. You need some air. You over worked today?"

"Nope."

"Scott, you never told me your age." "Why? I'm 30."

"Do you know how old am I?"

"You must be in your twenties."

"I just turned twenty. We have a serious age difference, and we don't seem to be agreeing on anything. You are taking too much control of me, and you're not being fair."

"You complain too much."

"No! Be honest, are you only dating me, or you have other girlfriends around?"

"I have."

"Define."

"I go out with girls."

"And you're dating me?"

"Yes. You're my girl."

"Also?"

"Yeah, but I care for you the most."

"So, is that why you lied for a couple of days?"
"No, I said I had business to do."

"With who?"

"You don't need to know."

"No, I really don't!" I raised my voice. I'm really getting emotional.

"How's James by the way? You go out with him too?"

"He is my friend."

"Ok."

"I'm going to say goodbye and one day when you are really old enough and acting your age, you will understand why I'm doing this."

"You're dumping me, eh?" he said it with an evil voice.

"Yeah, since you play masked, it should be your turn to see how it feels to be dumped."

"Hey, I'm honest, but there are some things that are improper to say."

"Bye."

"Excuse me? Next time no child like you will be in my picture."

"You will be in a picture all right, but alone. Without that twenty four hour business suit, you would be worth nothing."

I closed the phone and got so frustrated because of that fake! I was so mad! I threw my pillow on the floor. I was sobbing for a bit, until I felt better.

An hour later, I went downstairs to the kitchen. I saw my whole family finishing their supper at the dining room table. Hayley wasn't there.

"Mom, why didn't you call me for supper?"

"I heard you were on the phone, so I did not bother you."

"Thanks."

"What's up hun?" dad asked, as he brought his plate in the kitchen.

"Nothing."

"School's ok?"

"Yeah."

"You're home on a Friday? Why don't you go out?"

"Too tired."

"Ok."

There were left over mashed potatoes, and roasted carrots. I heated them in the oven, while getting my plate and my drink ready.

"Mom, when is Hayley coming home?"

"Later on tonight before midnight."

I didn't want to talk to her, just spill tears beside her, and have the everything is going to be ok scene.

My supper was ready. I took a plate, and filled it with everything, took my glass of water, went to the living room table, and ate quickly.

I said my good nights to my parents after that, and went upstairs. I won't wait for Hayley tonight, instead, I will write in my journal, pouring out my emotions.

Journal,

Everything is back to what it was before the sun was set, on that Saturday afternoon, when I met that what's his face character. I'm feeling relieved, and overjoyed with emotions.

I need some light, while I sleep.

I turned on my lava lamp, and stared at the purple liquid, until I dozed off.

Almost home

Saturday has come, my caving to oversleep in bed was essential. I opened my eyes, and saw Hayley sleeping, on the bed next to mine.

I got up slowly, and went to the bathroom to take a nice bath, and wash my hair. When there are events like today, I like to take my time pampering myself.

I'm occupied cleansing my face, washing my hair, and body.

By the time everything is done, it will already be noon.

Hayley woke up by my chaotic search for something to wear, from our closet.

"Problem?" she asked.

"Yeah, I need to find something to wear for the first show, at the don't know the name yet theater today."

 "Oh, really? I would not mind seeing it. Can David and I come too?"

"Yeah, you should arrange it with Syd, and for sure they'll let you in. Be there by four, the show starts at four-thirty"

Hayley got out of her bed.

She walked over to the closet, and looked at the clothes. "You need something sexy," she said.

"I'm not the sexy type, you know that. I need something classic."

"Classic? But you need to live up your feminine giving."

"For whom?"

"Everyone and including you."

"I'm not a you know what."

"Who said you are, you won't dress like that. Just leave this to me."

I trust her, I see the way she wardrobes herself in the most noticeable way. I dress cute, but too everyday.

Hayley got busy on that after she dressed, and then called Syd, and confirmed David about the show, while I was curling my hair. The show is at four-thirty, and then the after party begins in the evening. I know it's too early to dress, but there are plenty of things to do.

The phone rang, I picked up.

"Hello?"

"Hey, it's Celia."

"Hey, what's up?

"Not much, are you getting ready?"

"Yes, my sister and David are coming too. It's going to be fun!"

"You sound happy. I won't even ask what happened last night, because I'm already sensing everything went as planned. Antonio and I will pick you up by three o'clock, Syd and James will be already at the theater by two."

"All right, all right, mission did accomplish."

The memory of last night passed through my head, and then I came back to my normal conscience.

"Oh, I felt like it was a waste, but I did it." I told her. "Well then, you shall continue life."

"Yeah, see you later."

"Bye."

The phone automatically hanged up.

I was done curling my hair, and my outfit was ready to be worn. Of course, it's one of Hayley's styles. It's a golden top with light red beads around my waist. I'll be wearing a black-layered skirt, and black thin heeled laced sandals to match with it. Hayley wanted to do my make up. She smoked my eyes, glittered around my eyelids, and thickened my lips with a sandy-peachy metallic color. She bronzed my cheeks, my arms, and a bit on my legs. I have tanned in two minutes. Sillly.

"You are still naturel without surgery," she said, while painting me with the make up. I was her white canvas, and she will paint me with colors.

"I'm just me with make up."

"You look hot!" she yelled out loud.

"You know who I look like Hayley?"

I was tapping my left foot, while looking at the mirror and noticing my reflection did not describe of me anymore.

"Who?" she said.

"Not me."

"Nah, you look sexy."

I didn't say anything. I looked at the pink rectangle clock next to my bed, and saw it was almost time to go.

Hayley finished the makeup. She suggested me to wear a nice bracelet with a ring, or a necklace. I didn't bother wearing a necklace, but I wore my loopy gold earrings instead. I took out my little black purse from the closet, and added things in it to bring with me. I wore my long soft beige jacket, and did some last touch ups on my hair in front of the mirror.

"Anyway, I'm going to go downstairs, and wait for Antonio and Celia," I said.

"I'll see you there, I'll tell the parents we'll be out late together."

"Thanks for everything." I said, and went downstairs in the living room, to wait for my ride.

Old Montreal

There was a clanky beep from outside, my ride was already there.

I went outside, and walked straight to Antonio's car. I sat at the backseat. I heard an "Aww!" from Celia.

I started to giggle.

"You got a hot date tonight?" Antonio asked.

It always comes to that saying when someone sees you dressed differently, and then my turn comes, and I say,

"Yeah." as a joke.

Antonio started to drive in the theater's direction.

I'm the only one without a date tonight. Syd must be thinking the same way.

"You need a nice boyfriend." Antonio suggested. "Where can I find one?" I said sarcastically.

"Somewhere, at the right time."

"Syd is alone too tonight." I said.

"No, he's not, he's bringing himself, and he doesn't need to reserve an extra seat for it."

Antonio laughed too hard on his joke.

Four o'clock had arrived. The parking was always a problem.

The theater is on a street called Le Royer in the Old Montreal area, and it looked very polished. James will be doing his first performance without any plays, or other bands.

When we got inside, our first impression was that, it did not look like a theater, it was more like a party with plenty of people, and decorations all over the place. Still, it was quite a turn out.

"Where did he find all these people?" I asked. "From his mouth." Antonio replied.

He was being silly. He really wants Syd to trip one day.

I walked towards a long table, filled with delicious appetizers, and drinks for all the guests.

"Look all the stuff!" Celia shouted, as she eyed the food on the table. She did get everyone's attention.

"Where are all the real drinks?" I asked.

"I think that's for after the show. They must have a bar around here. Syd is cookoo, if he doesn't have one." Antonio replied.

"Wow, Lynna you're sizzling tonight!" Syd popped out of nowhere.

"Well, you look interesting too." I said.

He's wearing the tightest clothes you could ever find. He's dressed in a black top, with black polyester pants, black shoes, and crazy gold chains hanging on his neck like a disco king. This is his daily wardrobe.

"Spiffy cologne you're wearing." I added.

"Thanks."

This guy is always ready to go dancing. He probably sleeps in his clothes too. When he hears the alarm from his clock, he jumps into his car, and goes to his circus.

"It's great the three of you could make it." Syd said. "Ha, ha!" Antonio laughed.

"Where's James?" I asked.

"I believe he's backstage getting ready. Don't get lost, you need to stay with me, so that we can sit together."

I thought of going backstage, and surprising him, but perhaps it's better off to see him on stage.

We went to the reserved seats near the stage. Syd had already been sitting in the middle.

"Who's the monkey?" Antonio mumbled.

Celia and I didn't even bother saying anything.

"Oh, here, I forgot about the pamphlets I made." Syd handed them to us when we sat beside him.

"You made them? I never knew you're creative." I said.

The theme looked great, there are red petals on the front page, it must be a symbol of today's event.

"I am artistic sometimes…" He was the only one who started to laugh.

I had a funny smile on my face, the other two were staring at him, as if he's really a monkey.

I'm surprised he hasn't hit on Celia yet. Celia hasn't said a word.

Syd has always something to say to get her irritated, and if it were to happen, he'll get it from Antonio.

"Syd, why aren't you playing something tonight?" Antonio asked.

"I'm too shy."

"Shy, huh?"

Hayley and David had arrived, Hayley sat beside me, and David sat on the last reserved seat next to Hayley.

Syd was sitting on the other side beside me, Antonio beside him, and Celia was in the corner.

Syd handed the genuine pamphlets to them.

"Aren't these your favorites?" Hayley whispered into my ear. "Yeah, but red petals exist?" I asked.

"Yes, for special occasions.

"Lynna you look different." David said.

"Hayley transformed me to someone else." "She did a good job."

"Thank you." Hayley said, with a sweet voice.

The lights dimmed and the crowd started yelling, whistling, and clapping.

Music spread across the whole theater. The spotlight lit on the drummer, they shouted his name, and then to the base player, and finally James, the guitar player.

"Yeah, James, woohoo!" Syd yelled.

"Yeah, James." I said. I don't think anyone heard me.

"Hey, everyone! Welcome to the EternalCryzz Theater, named by the first band performing here today. Is it time to rock or what!" Tod, the bass player announced proudly.

"EternalCryzz Theater?" I whispered, "Cool."

"We wouldn't be performing this night, if it weren't for Sydrick, if only we knew where he is sitting today."

"He's right here!" I yelled, as I was pointing at him. What power came in me? Must be the top I'm wearing.

The bass player saw my reaction.

"There he is!" he said. "Thanks pretty one!" I got all red.

"Sydbaby come say hello to the people." He was nodding no.

"Come on!"

He walked over to the stage, and came in front of the microphone.

I felt a quick feeling of heat through my body, when James spotted me, I looked down until the redness on my face disappeared.

"Ahem!" Syd cleared his throat, and he continued.

"Thanks for the speech Tod. I am happy to open this theater. My parents gave me this place. I told them what I would like to be when I grow up, and they took me seriously."

Some in the audience were laughing.

"We should remember this day as a gift given to me, and I have given it to you. It has been helpful when my best friend James, as you know the guitar player, gave time to teach me to work hard, and organize myself today."

He kept on going and going about himself for another ten minutes. I assumed he would say James will be his partner, but he looked too tangled on his own web, and couldn't get out of it.

He continued until he had nothing else to say about himself. The band looked eager to start playing. I was rolling my eyes, and getting tired of the speech.

"Come on man, quit it!" someone yelled from the back.

"Did you say there is a party after this?" David asked Hayley and I. "Yes." I said

"Ah, it will really be a late one."

Everyone always has a comment on Syd. I don't know why. I still need to have the talk with James.

Hesitation was around. I wanted to get up and go for a walk, just anywhere, but everyone is seated, and if I did leave, people's eyes would be staring at me.

There was clapping. Syd's speech was finally over.

The music started, and everyone just got wild. The rhythm of the music became stronger. This lasted for a while.

It was great.

It's the end of the show and everyone walked next door, where the party is. The food is refilled, and the real drinks are ready to be served.

I had to be the follower tonight, since I didn't have a date. I was following Celia and Antonio, but then I noticed that they were going to a corner, to be alone. I walked at the bar, where Hayley and David are.

"Hey," Hayley said.

"You want a drink?"

"Nah."

"Lynna, come sit and have a drink with us." David said.

I did, but I felt a little uncomfortable sitting on a stool, crossing my legs with this skirt on.

The disco music kept on changing every five minutes.

Mr. Syd looked too cool for school, and flirted with some girls he met at the bar.

"A pink lady please!" I yelled at the bar person.

A minute later, I got my pink lady. I was stirring it with a funny looking toothpick, and then ended off to another world.

"Hey!" I heard David yelling. "Good show."

"We are thrilled to be here." Hayley said.

"Thanks, it's great that everyone is here to support me, and the band. Syd had some speech there too, very long and educative."

"Tell me about it, he was like a choochoo train, must've had problems with his breaks." David said.

"Yeah, that's my buddy. Anyway have fun, see you later."

"Later."

I heard a "hi." I looked up, and saw James.

"Hey." I saw that Hayley and David had left, while I was daydreaming. He sat beside me.

He looked into my eyes, and smiled.

"You're always calm and mellow."

"Yeah, so?" I said. I just had a drink.

He didn't answer.

"Hey, man, a beer please!" He shouted at the bar guy.

Why do we yell at bartenders?

"Ok" he said, as he read the sign.

The banner says everything is free.

We didn't have to pay for anything.

James turned his head around, back to me, and watched me sip my drink. "Thanks." he said, to the bar guy, when he got his bottle of beer.

"Did you like the show?" he asked.

"Yes."

I didn't want to talk, I felt something, a feeling I had in me, years back, if you know what I mean. I did feel safe. He's dressed nicely. He's wearing black pants, a light gray shirt, and a red baseball cap, seriously.

"Are baseball caps allowed to wear at a party?" I asked.

 "I'll take it off for you."

He did, but it didn't matter.

He had his arms crossed, and leaned on the table. "How about the discussion." I said.

"I would like that."

Meanwhile, appetizers and champagne were being served. People are taking pictures.

"But not here, we should go somewhere quiet. We will do this later. You have the time?" I asked.

"Yeah."

David came back to our spot, he had his camera in his hands, and asked if he can take a picture of James and I.

"Thanks." he said, took the picture and left.

"Where is your camera today?" James asked.

I am addicted in taking photos, but I couldn't bring my camera today. I felt too dressed up and felt was enough to bring.

"At home." I said.

"Ok hey, let's go have the talk." he suggested.

He took my hand to help me get off from the stool and let go. We left our drinks there. People ran to him for interviews and photos.

"Ok let's go." he said as the people vanished.

We walked to find a quiet place.

"I had more interviews with my band before I came to see you. It's unbelievable."

"You're going to be famous!" I said

"I know Lynna, perhaps in a couple of years I'll be touring around the place."

We walked to the entrance of the theater and sat on the long wooden black bench beside the window.

It had started to rain, it looked beautiful.

"It's too bad my mom is not here to see this."

James lives with his mom. His parents separated when he was five years old and then moved next door. His mom went to visit his grandparents, because his grandmother isn't feeling too well, and she had to be there.

"Hey pictures would be wonders. When she comes back you will show them to her and make her feel she was here." I tried to cheer him up.

"Ha, ha, ok. Did I tell you, you look very nice tonight?"

"No you did not."

"Your eyes are glowing like kryptonite."

"Thanks superman."

"I sing, play music, go out and be wild, but I don't know how to tell you the way I think or feel. If no one talks, I just continue walking on my road.

 I know I should always look ways to open up."

"Go on."

"Let's go back to a decade when we were about twelve years old."

"You mean that summer?"

"Yes, it just happened, my hormones were awake and sensed you around."

"Ok." I said.

"What I did know back then, we were growing up and it was leading up to somewhere."

"Was that cool with you?" I asked.

Really what was he talking about, it sounded like something he was trying to describe.

"It was an experience. You are cute Lynna, you know that, in those years seeing you grow up and becoming different, made me want to know you more."

I blushed.

"Remember the other summer?" he asked.

I did remember it very well.

It was the summer before our senior year, things were different. We went on dates and I got to understand him in his adolescent phase. He was wild person.

"Yes I do!"

"I went on a downfall."

"Why did you stop climbing?"

"I don't know, I really don't know." he was saying it very seriously.

"Were you scared?" I asked.

"I guess."

"James?"

"Yes."

"You can't release it can you?"

"Release what?"

"Your feelings the truth!"

I don't think he knew how to unless he tried.

He put his arm around me, to keep warm.

"I was afraid and I had to let you go," he said.

"We split for this? We should've talked about it then."

"Yeah, but I felt that it was too late, you know, you had some guys after you."

"You had that crazy basketball player."

That crazy basketball player was in the girl's team at school, she wanted to win and be better than the other players.

"You saw the way that girl used me until I was crushed into pieces."

"Yeah, that was childish."

"Whatever it was, it has vanished."

He stood up and took my left hand to help get up from the bench.

On a windy rainy evening, it feels warm.

He came closer to me, took my hands and reached to kiss my right cheek.

"You're still in my heart even though we've been our separate ways. It would've been different, if I didn't know the Lynna in my life."

It is a beautiful summer morning, I went to my bedroom window and saw him. I waved and said "I'll be right there!"

Domicile